Baking Day!

Adapted by Natalie Shaw

Based on the screenplay "Baking Mistakes"
written by Becky Friedman

Poses and layouts by Jason Fruchter

Ready-to-Read

Simon Spotlight
New York London Toronto Sydney New Delhi

SIMON SPOTLIGHT
An imprint of Simon & Schuster Children's Publishing Division
1230 Avenue of the Americas, New York, New York 10020
This Simon Spotlight edition August 2021
© 2021 The Fred Rogers Company. All rights reserved.
All rights reserved, including the right of reproduction in whole or in part in any form.
SIMON SPOTLIGHT, READY-TO-READ, and colophon are registered trademarks of Simon & Schuster, Inc.
For information about special discounts for bulk purchases, please contact Simon & Schuster
Special Sales at 1-866-506-1949 or business@simonandschuster.com.
Manufactured in the United States of America 0721 LAK
2 4 6 8 10 9 7 5 3 1
ISBN 978-1-5344-9508-1 (hc)
ISBN 978-1-5344-9507-4 (pbk)
ISBN 978-1-5344-9509-8 (ebook)

"Hi, neighbor!
We are helping
Baker Aker today,"
Daniel Tiger said.

"We are going to bake cookies!" said Prince Wednesday.

They both wanted to make cookies shaped like Trolley!

Baker Aker had a recipe.

Prince Wednesday started to dance as he added the sugar.

Oh no.
He bumped into
the table
and spilled the milk!

Prince Wednesday
cleaned up
while Daniel got
more milk.

"Now we mix," said Baker Aker.

Soon they had dough!
They rolled it out.

Baker Aker gave them cookie cutters shaped like trolleys.

They made the cookies
and placed them
on a baking sheet.

Then Daniel dropped
a cookie!
"How do I fix it?"
he asked.

"You can mix it back in with your dough to make a new cookie," Baker Aker said.

Baker Aker put the cookies in the oven.

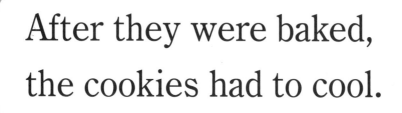

After they were baked,
the cookies had to cool.

To fix the mistake,
he used round candies
to make new wheels!

Soon the cookies looked like Trolley!

Decorate your own cookies!

Hi, neighbor! Do you like baking cookies at home? One of the best parts of making cookies is decorating them! Ask a grown-up for help and decorate your cookies to look just like me, Daniel Tiger! All you need to do is add colorful stripes and whiskers to round cookies.

Ugga Mugga!